Naughty Nicky

This book is a presentation of
Weekly Reader Children's Book Club.

Weekly Reader Children's Book Club
offers book clubs for children from
preschool through junior high school.
For further information write to:
Weekly Reader Children's Book Club
4343 Equity Drive
Columbus, Ohio 43228

First published in the United States in 1983 by
Holt, Rinehart and Winston, 383 Madison Avenue,
New York, New York 10017.

Originally published in Great Britain under the title
Naughty Nigel by Andersen Press Ltd.

Library of Congress Cataloging in Publication Data

Ross, Tony.
Naughty Nicky.

Summary: Naughty Nicky always pretends to misunder-
stand as an excuse to do dreadful things.
[1. Behavior—Fiction] I. Title.
PZ7.R71992Nau   1983   [E]   82-21265
ISBN: 0-03-063522-5

First American Edition

Printed in Italy
1   3   5   7   9   10   8   6   4   2

WEEKLY READER CHILDREN'S BOOK CLUB presents

Naughty Nicky

TONY ROSS

Holt, Rinehart and Winston
New York

Naughty Nicky thought he could do anything he wanted. Whenever he was asked to do something he hated, he would pretend not to hear properly. Then he would do just what he wanted, instead. His parents *thought* he was trying to be good, but that his ears didn't work very well.

The best head doctor in the world couldn't find anything wrong with Nicky's ears.

This is the sort of thing Nicky did:

On Monday, his father asked him to "wash the dishes."

"Yes, Dad," said Nicky. Away he went, and nobody saw him again until the evening. When Nicky came into the kitchen to give the cat its supper, his father asked about the dishes.

"Oh," said Nicky. "I thought you said wash the *fishes*. That's what I've done, but they weren't very dirty!"

Father felt rather sorry for Nicky and his ears that didn't work properly.

On Tuesday, Nicky had to go to the dentist, who wanted to make a hole in his teeth, then fill it in again.

"Get your hat," said Mother, who was going to take him to the bus. After two hours' searching, she found Nicky in an upstairs corner with his paint set.

Mother was angry, because it was too late for the dentist, and she shouted at Nicky.

"I'm sorry, Mom," he said. "I thought you said *paint the cat.*"

Mother felt very sorry for Nicky and his sleepy ears.

Nicky was naughty on Wednesday and Thursday and
Friday too. It was a lovely week.

When asked to dust the stairs, he went to the zoo to
bust the bears. Well, they were too big to bust, so
he teased them terribly instead.

He had lots of fun doing all of his favorite bad things.

All the time, the grown-ups said how sorry they felt
because of his ears, and they gave him little presents.

On Saturday, Nicky went to play in the woods. His parents had told him, "Be home by *seven*."

"Hmm," thought Nicky. "I think I heard them say *eleven*." So Nicky stayed out very late. So late, that he began to doze under a tree.

Then strange things began to happen. The trees around him seemed to move and change color. Strange animals popped out of the ground, and Nicky didn't know if he was awake or asleep. A strange little man came skipping along the path.

The little man seemed friendly and he spoke in a squeaky voice: "Hello, welcome to Nightland. This is where dreams come true. I'm in charge." He peeped into a tiny red book. "You're Nicky, yes? What would you like—magic, money, your wildest dreams?"

The little man seemed to be in a frightful hurry, and his words tumbled out. Nicky was so surprised he couldn't think of a single wish. The little man hopped from foot to foot. "Hurry, boy, I haven't got all night!"

Still, it was a chance too good to miss, and Nicky blurted out the first thing that came into his head. "I wish...er...I had, er, a...errr...*golden rose.*"

There was a puff of striped smoke, and *something* happened. Nicky had a huge golden *nose*. It was so huge he could see it without a mirror, and it was extremely heavy.

The little man listened to Nicky's cries. "I'm sorry," he murmured. "I thought you said a golden nose. Never mind, you may make another wish." This time Nicky knew exactly what to ask for. "I wish my nose was the way it was before."

"Granted," said the little man.

Nicky touched his nose. It was still long and glossy. Then he noticed his feet.

"What have you done?" he shrieked. "I wanted my nose to be the way it was before!"

The little man frowned. "I'm *so* sorry," he said sadly. "I thought you said you wanted your *toes* to cover more of the *floor*. Never mind, you can make another wish."

Nicky stared at his monstrous feet over his golden nose and said carefully: "I wish my feet were just an ordinary pair."

Nicky watched his feet, and to his horror, they began to turn brown and hairy.

"What's happening?" he sobbed. "All I wanted was an ordinary pair of feet."

"*Pair*?" said the little man, smiling. "Sorry, I thought you said *bear*. Never mind, you can make another wish."

"No thanks," gasped Nicky through his tears. "Things are getting worse and worse."

Sobbing into his soggy brown fur, he fled blindly into the Nightland forest.

Nicky stumbled on, not noticing the way the Nightland changed into the ordinary world he was used to.

Dawn was just breaking as he arrived home. As quiet as a mouse, he crept into bed. He felt uncomfortable, because his pajamas didn't fit. Tucking his golden nose under the blankets, he tried to sleep.

All he could think about was what his friends would say when he went to school. They would laugh at a bear with big feet and a long golden nose.

The next morning, Nicky rushed to the mirror, to find that he was his old, ordinary self again.

He was so happy, he spent the day doing not-so-very-naughty things. In the afternoon, his father came into the garden where Nicky was playing with the cat.

"Would you go to the forest and collect some logs?" said Father.

Nicky had a wonderfully, gloriously, naughty idea. He would pretend he thought his father said, "Collect *dogs*." Then he would fill the garden with dozens of dogs.

"Yes, Dad," said Nicky.

But on the way to the forest, Nicky remembered his dream about Nightland and the little man who misunderstood everything. He suddenly realized that it wasn't nice to pretend to mix things up.

So when he got to the forest, he changed his mind. He didn't collect *dogs*, he collected *logs*.